This book belongs to:

LAKEVIEW ELEMENTARY SCHOOL LIBRARY
MAHOPAC, NEW YORK 10541

P9-DNW-605

LAKEVIEW ELEMENTARY SCHOOL LIBRARY
MAHOPAC, NEW YORK 10541

SLIM and MISS PRIM

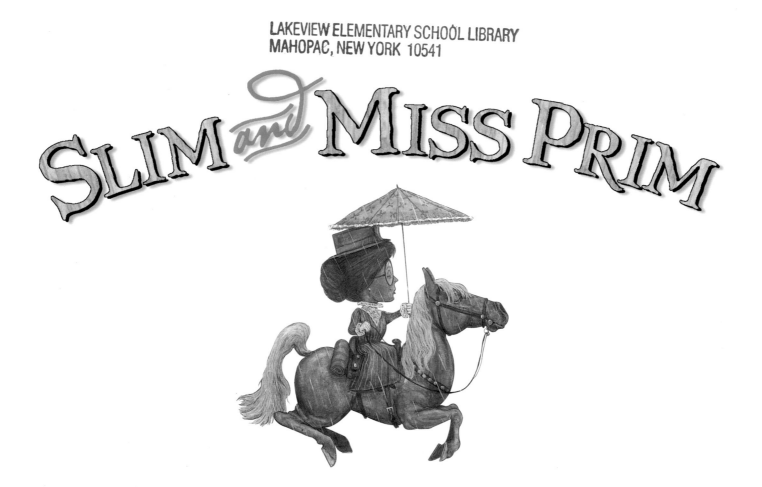

by ROBERT KINERK

illustrations by JIM HARRIS

rising moon

Books for Young Readers from Northland Publishing

The illustrations were done in watercolor on bristol board
The display and text type were set in Trump Mediaeval
Composed in the United States of America
Designed by Jennifer Schaber
Edited by Stephanie Bucholz
Production Supervised by Lisa Brownfield

Printed in Hong Kong by South Sea International Press Ltd.

Copyright © 1998 by Robert Kinerk
Illustrations copyright © 1998 by Jim Harris
All rights reserved.

This book may not be reproduced in whole or in part, by any means (with the
exception of short quotes for the purpose of review), without permission of
the publisher. For information, address Northland Publishing Company, P.O.
Box 1389, Flagstaff, AZ 86002-1389.

First Impression
ISBN 0-87358-689-1

Kinerk, Robert.
Slim and Miss Prim / by Robert Kinerk ; illustrated by Jim Harris.
p. cm.
Summary: When rustlers capture the talkative Marigold Prim, her cattle,
and her ranch hand, they find her incessant conversation too much to
bear and change their plans.
ISBN 0-87358-689-1
[1. Robbers and outlaws—Fiction. 2. Cowboys—Fiction. 3. Stories in
rhyme.] I. Harris, Jim, 1955–   ill. II. Title.
PZ8.3.K566S1 1998   98-6943
[Fic—dc21]

0633/7.5M/9-98

For Anne Warner.

— R. K.

On a ranch near the mountains a cowboy named Slim
worked for a lady named Marigold Prim.
He mended her fences and herded her cattle
and listened at length to Marigold's prattle.

Cowboys on ranches all over the state
said it was awful. They said they would hate
working for someone who droned on and on,
morning, and evening, and noontime, and dawn.
They said, "All that talk, Slim, it must drive you mad."
But Slim only smiled. He said, "It's not bad."

In herding the cattle and rounding up strays
Slim often went riding for days and for days,
and if you had followed him out on the range
you would have heard something that may have seemed strange.
With prairie dogs barking and hawks high above,
Slim played his guitar and sang songs of love.

In the hills near the prairie where the herd loved to tramp,
a rustler band had a well-hidden camp.
"Listen," their boss said, a large man named Lee,
"I think I hear singing, slightly off-key.
Go have a look, boys. I can't help but feel
this may be a ranch hand with cows we can steal."

Clippety-cloppety, off went his gang
on the track of the cowboy who rode and who sang.
Down from the mountains and over the dunes,
they found him at last by his loudly sung tunes.
They plugged up their ears and fought a brief battle,
then kidnapped poor Slim and stole all his cattle.

"Slim," Lee explained in camp the next day,
"Now that you're here, I'm afraid you must stay.
You'd blab to the sheriff if we set you free.
You'd snitch to the sheriff, and it's clear to me
the next thing you know—in a wink—without fail—
me and my boys would be thrown into jail."

Slim fretted and fumed. He paced back and forth.
He tried riding south. He tried riding north.
But each time he tried it a rustler guard
would make him go back and sit in the yard.
Where he sat . . . and he sat . . . day after day,
through March, and through April, and on into May.

Miss Marigold Prim in the meantime, of course,
had put on her hat and saddled her horse.
She said, "I'm not worried. At least not a lot.
But it seems to me likely a good cowboy ought
not be absent for seventeen weeks with no word.
I'm concerned about Slim, not to mention the herd."

She rode through the counties of Lincoln and Clark.
She rode in the daylight. She rode in the dark.
She buttonholed strangers and said to them sternly,
in Caselton, Carp, Caliente, and Fernley,
"Slim and my cattle—you've seen them, I hope?"
Each person she askcd, however, said, "Nope."

On she went riding, through Lander and Nye,
questioning, searching, until, by and by,
word reached the hideout of Lee and his bunch,
and Lee, who was eating, said, "Boys, I've a hunch
that this could mean trouble, so here's what to do:
ride out there and capture Miss Marigold, too."

Clippety-cloppety, off went his bunch
and captured Miss Prim, who had stopped to have lunch.
Then back to the hideout, cloppety-clip,
after, of course, they had stolen the tip.

"This is unheard of!" Miss Prim said to Lee.
"First you grab Slim and then you grab me!"
She lectured him sternly. She'd lots more to say.
She lectured, in fact, the rest of the day,
and early that evening, while eating their stew,
she repeated her talk for the sake of his crew.

Next morning at six, or shortly before,
while the gang was at breakfast, she lectured some more.

She lectured on manners, she lectured on crime,
the importance of keeping appointments on time,
brushing your teeth after breakfast and dinner,
the foods you should eat to help you get thinner,
how to darn sox and how to mend pants,
covering food to keep out the ants,
the names of the flowers you'd see by the path,
how horrible you smell when you don't take a bath.

She lectured them daily. She lectured them nightly.
They listened and listened and listened. Politely
at first, then a strain started showing.
Some drummed with their fingers and some started going,
"Ahem," or "Harrumph," or clearing their throats,
or glancing at watches, or reaching for coats,

and climbing out windows and sneaking out doors,
or saying, "Excuse me, I have to do chores."
Some saddled up horses and, leaping on top,
raced away screeching,"Marigold, STOP!"

They finally told Lee (they were nearly in tears),
"This could go on, boss, for years and for years.
For your sake, for our sake," they pleaded, "for peace,
we think you should offer Miss Prim her release."

They saddled her horse. They said, "You can go."
She said, "Nothing doing. Ridiculous. No.
You fellows are silly. That's sad but it's true.
I'm not leaving here unless Slim can come, too."

And Slim, when they told him, said he'd agree,
but only if all the cows were set free.
He said as a cowboy he'd given his word
he'd always watch out for Miss Marigold's herd.

The rustlers pleaded. They begged and they cried.
They pouted and sulked. But they finally complied.

They gave them the cows, and a lunch for the ride.
Then Marigold Prim, with Slim at her side
and hundreds of cattle all going, "Moo, moo,"
shouted goodbye to Lee and his crew.

Hip-hip-hooray, then! And off they went riding,
Yip-yip-a-yaying and ki-yi-yi-yiding,
herding the cattle across the wide plain,
herding the cattle through sunshine and rain.
Rounding up strays by shouting and yelling
and making their way to Miss Marigold's dwelling.

And after all this, as you might have supposed,
Slim gathered his courage, and knelt, and proposed.

Friends galloped in whooping from near and away
to dance and to sing on their wedding day.

Now out on the range, with hawks high above,
Slim still tends the cattle and sings songs of love.
Though when the wind's right and his duties permit,
he'll stop what he's doing. He'll stop and he'll sit
and listen in hopes the breezes are bringing
the faraway sound of some faraway singing.
For back on the ranch the former Miss Prim
is singing as well: a love song to Slim.

 **ROBERT KINERK** grew up in the little fishing town of Ketchikan in southeastern Alaska. He has worked as a newspaper reporter and has written stories and plays all his life. One of his plays, *The Fish Pirate's Daughter,* is still regularly performed in his home town for tourists every summer.

Robert is a graduate of Santa Clara University and also attended the University of Notre Dame. He and his wife have two children, Chevy and Alice. Through reading to them every night in their childhood years, Robert developed a love for children's stories.

His interest in cowboys came from rainy-day matinees at the Revilla Theater in Ketchikan, and from an oil painting that was a gift to his grandfather, a gold miner in Montana, and his grandmother, a school teacher there, on their wedding day almost a hundred years ago. In the painting, a pony express rider gallops over the western plains.

Robert and his family now live in Manchester, New Hampshire.

 **JIM HARRIS** has been an artist since the age of four, but has been paid for it since 1981.

In addition to *The Three Little Javelinas,* Jim Harris has illustrated many popular children's books, including *The Tortoise and the Jackrabbit* (written by Susan Lowell) and *Jack and the Giant: A Story Full of Beans* (written by himself), both from Rising Moon, as well as *Ten Little Dinosaurs* and *Mystery in Bugtown* (Accord Publishing Ltd.).

Jim has also illustrated printed materials for a diverse group of clients such as *Ranger Rick* and *Sesame Street* magazines and the National Wildlife Foundation.

Among Jim's honors and awards are a silver medal from the New York Society of Illustrators and an Award for Excellence from *Communication Arts* magazine.

Jim lives with his wife, Marian, and their children at the end of a winding dirt road near Mesa, Colorado.